By DiTales

A Word from the Author

This is a journey into my mind, my thoughts, feelings, and the questions that arrest my soul. It is an attempt to extend my conversations with myself beyond myself. I am inviting you to witness and participate in my monologue, so that it becomes a dialogue. I hope that you find something here, something just for you.

Table of Contents

QUESTIONS

What is it that matters?
The truth? Or compromise?
Does it get easier?

Life is a movie.
What's the structure?
How does it end?

Would you rather be a slave to the
desires of the self?
Or controlled by the demands of
the world?

Do we live for the future?
Or through our knowledge of the past?

Many ways that life can be lived, how is one ever sure, that her way of life is *her* way, to live?

Are people homeless because of
their choices?
Or because of fate?

You ever just randomly remember that you're in a body?

It just hit me, that I'm me, in a body, that I carry everywhere and introduce as myself.

How do I love?
While not sure of what love requires
of me?

I wonder what it all means.
What is it all for?
What we do it, for?
Why we gotta do it, for?
What's the point, of it all?

Life is such a maze.
Nothing makes sense.
We are always caught between worlds
of contrasting,
Yet, equal desires.
We are never content.
But we can't help it.
What now?
Where to, now?
Who now?
Nothing.
What if, it's for,
Nothing.

What if nothing matters at the end of it all?

What if existence is a purely coincidental occurrence without a purpose?

THE PAST

One should not live in the past,
It's filled with regret, they say.
But they also say:
One needs to know
where they've been
To know where they're going.
What then?
How can we do one without the other?
When doing one invites the other.
What is the way out?

InSAnity

MOMENTS

HEAVY IS THE SOUL

She rests on the floor.
The weight of her body,
Sinking into the ground.
"I just wanna leave it all on the floor,"
she says.
She can only try, for a moment.

THE LADY

I asked a lady:
"Are you okay?"
She replied,
"Yeah, I'm just old."

STEPHAN

"What the fuck is going on!" He says.
I respond:
"Nobody knows! We're all just
winging it."
He lets it go, tries to anyway, realizing…
He'll never get a sufficient answer.
The party goes on.

SURVIVAL MODE

Sometimes it was hard, to go on, felt
like I was wasting away, collecting dust,
A waste of "God's gift to the world."
Tried not to pay it much attention,
because that made it harder to carry
on… But carrying on, felt like a betrayal
of self.

OH, MY DAYS

They're limited...

I DON'T KNOW

I don't know, I don't know what's next,
or what should be next.

Is there more to life than working to pay
bills and getting drunk?

And "forgetting" what we can't forget?

I should sleep. It is 1:42 AM,
Nov 6, 2022.

I have just gotten back from work, and I
am very tired.

I'm also quite unsure about a lot
of things.

And I don't know.

THE DAZE OF THE DAYS

I OFTEN

I often replay old moments and
memories in my head.
I try to imagine all the ways I could've
done things differently…
But the show must go on.

ME VS ME

Sometimes I look at myself,
And I can't recognize myself
But I don't even know,
What I'm supposed to recognize.

THOUGHTS

All these thoughts, circling inside
of me,
I just wanna be free.
I wanna live
Like I want to
Like I need to
To feel, alive.

VOICES

All the voices that have
Created me
Molded me.
If only they could
Leave,
For me
To be, alone
Let me, be
Let me, decide
Let me, discover
My history
My future
Create, my forever.

12AM

Here, by myself.
Embodying the weight of my existence,
All by myself,
Trying to be myself,
All of myself,
Need to be myself,
To be myself.
It's all about the self,
But the self is never alone.
Caught in transition,
Floating no floater.
Sinking,
Eternal.

TWO WORLDS

Imagine.
The difference
Between your ideal reality,
And your current reality.
How do you feel?

SOMETIMES

Sometimes, I wish I couldn't think,
Cause thinking, breeds my InSAnity.

Thinking, tears me apart

Scatters me

I try to recoup but it,
Seduces me
Grips me...
I'm afraid I've got nothing left.

But I'm trying.
For what it's worth,
For all its worth.

It's gotta be worth something.

IMAGINE

Imagine.
Not being able to think,
Not being able to experience the
Conflicts of being human.
Some idea of freedom.

UNCERTAINTY

Just when you think you know,
you realize.
Knowledge is only valuable when
it's acknowledged.
So much to know, so much to forget.
Mystery looms at every corner,
Toying with the mind like a string,
toying with a Cat.
What becomes of us when we become
slaves to these mysteries?
Maybe, we become a mystery
to ourselves.
We become the string, and our minds,
The Cat.

PASSING THOUGHTS

I don't know what to make of my
life anymore.

Hard for me to see what my story is.
Amidst all my conflicts
and contradictions,
My pain.
But, there's beauty, too,
There's love,
There's care.

WHAT IS THERE

What is there?
Who knows.
You think you know
'Til something new comes along.
You think you feel
'Til the feeling fades.

Nothing lasts forever
Things move and we move with it,
Just keep moving,
Rain or shine,
Keep moving.

I LIED

I lied.
Scared of my own demons,
So I disguised them,
Fooling everyone.
But never fooling myself.

REMINISCING

Reminiscing.
The flavours of the present
bring relief, a moment of rescue.

Who can vouch for this rescue?
Or that its aftereffects remain
long enough.
Long enough to remain a moment
of rescue.

UNCOMFORTABLE

Rediscovering past joys
Noticing current pains,
Liberating self
To reclaim self
To connect self,
Letting go of expectations.

Surrender.

QUOTES

PASSING OF TIME

Past

        Present

                  Future   Past

     Present

Present.

ALL IN THE PRESENT

For the present.
The past,
The future,
Must give way.

TIME

Time will pass.
You just have to let it.

ANYTHING

Let anything happen,
It happens anyway.

TRANSITIONS

Walk into the future,
having fully experienced the past.

FREEDOM

Let your mind be free from the
shackles of your desires!

IDENTITY

As we are,
So we do.

YOU

What you are is enough.

WHAT YOU FEEL

Feel you
Be you
Live you.

You can't be all you wanna be for them,
If you're never what you need to be.
For YOU.

KNOWING

You don't know better until you
know better.
You don't know how better you
could know,
Until you
Know better.

You don't know what better is, until you
Know better!

How do you know what you can know,
Without exploring what there is
to know?

HUMAN

We're all so fragile.
In need of,
Just, in need of
Love.
Accept, our fragility.

EVERYONE

Everyone's tryna make sense of it,

Everyone's dying to figure it out,

Everyone.

BECOMING

BECOMING

Moving,

Craving silence, but moving, still.
Seeking to understand
It's never clear.

What's the truth?
What's the way ?

Routes
What's the destination?
Decisions
What's the outcome?
The answer?
Frail assumptions

Dying, only to
Revive
In another form
You're out of it,
But inside,
Trying to gain control.
A hopeless desire.

Calm,
Smile,
Keep on becoming.

UNSETTLED

Unsettled, drifting.
Moving, stopping
Only to begin again.

Still but urging for
Movement

Moving but urging for stillness

A moment, an end?

It slips away.

I drift, the chaos.

The never-ending urge for stillness
Longing for movement,

The process of becoming.
I embrace it.

BECOMING

Smile
Frown
Scream
Run
Walk
Crawl
Roll on the floor…

You're only trying to find your way.

InSAnity

MOTEL ADVENTURES

FLOW

I'm floating

Empty but full

Light,

Flowing

What is there?

What's the substance?

Craving isolation...

An urge to disconnect.

To discover.

Hopefully.

BLISSFUL STATE

Imagine nothingness.

Repetitive soundlessness.

In that state,
Unaffected,
Unmoved.
Observation only,
Eternal.

A PLACE

A place.
Quiet but loud

Anyone?

Nothing. Yet,

A voice…

Outside!

Run!

Alone.

Battling the demons inside.

Raging fire, cool surface.

ALL OF IT

I want all of it.
All the intensity.

I want it to rip me apart,
Caress me,
Obsess me,

Carry me away,
Make me lose control,

All of it.
All or nothing,
All or nothing.

WEIGHT

The vessel,
Alienated from the substance.
The substance,
Paralysed.

BEAT

Beat, beat, beat.

Hear the beating of the heart,

Feel the beating of the heart.

Listen,
When it calls
You must listen.
Or soon find your soul missing.

HELP

Help me
Lord!
I'm knowing but
Unknowing

Thinking but feeling

Running but stuck

Where?
What ?
When?
How?
How.

DAILY WALK

I'm walking again,
Contemplating my life.

The same thoughts and concerns
Runnin' through my mind,
Wondering when the cycle ends.

Waiting for the end
Looking for the end
For the answer.

The cure for this disease
That has hijacked my mind,
Spreading through my veins
Taking over my body
Heading towards my soul

How do stop it?
How do I end it?
Face the invisible Beast?

What is the way to the end?
Find the end.
Make it to the end.
Make it end.

HARMONY

Silence
Hear the mind speak.
It craves fluidity
A quality of the chameleon
Floating
Be-ing
An attitude of relaxation
Unshaken by
Momentary moments.

The journey ends
As it continues
Full stop

Silence.
That is the only way,
To hear the self.

InSAnity

A
MOMENT
IN THE
WOODS

ON A JOURNEY

A voyage, traveling, alone.
Desire to discover the true self,
The real thing,
To truly unleash it,
In its truest form.
Moments of silence,
Out of limited treasure.

SOLITUDE

Oh to be alone, peaceful.
Liberation.
When achieved, catharsis.
The door to unyielding
Authenticity, long delayed
By, banal everyday activities,
I am certain, that truth,
Approaches, when we disappear.
Only to truly love.

MONEY

A nonending menace.
Breathed into eternity by
Beings of limited existence.
A means of disguise,
Distraction rather,
From the rawness of reality
Money, scattered in multiple realms.
Lacking authority, but wielding power.
The epitome of a
bittersweet
Disaster.

RELATIONSHIPS

Essential, but poisonous.
Blissful mystery,
Stirred by action. Decided by fate.
No wonder, it is the heart of our pain.
But it remains, uninhibited
In its desirability.

SOCIETY

Labels, categories,
Numbers, places,
Suggestions, inferences, impediments.
Choice, make, choices, choose,
empty noises.
Time, make it before you, break.
Loose ends, marked tightly, deceit.
Be understood, be plain, be easy
Pick a lane, pick a side, choose,
your poison.
Just, make it easy, just tell us,
What we want to hear from you.
Whenever you choose. Take your time.
But watch the time, it works, for us.

NATURE

Clear, clean, pure
Ease, true, simplicity at its best.
Treasured, but only in its rarity,
Caused by our "sincerity."
At the end, it is all,
That remains.

OBSERVE

Watching the bikers bike,
The cars vroom!
They move, towards unending
destinations. Loud then quiet
Back to back, motion.
Explains it, we can't be still.
Because then, we, feel.
What a task, to understand what it
all means…
So, we move, into oblivion.

LOSE CONTROL

Sometimes, I just wanna lose control,
Unleash and separate my awareness of
caution. Of choice, of decision,
Of normalcy. Travel into a
nonexistent world where it's, only
Me. Living free.

DRIFTING

Tired of drifting
Shifting
Without a home.
Someone, find me a home.

My place in this place,
My happiness in this maze.

I hope it's only a phase,
Feels like a phase,
That never ends.

InSAnity

LOVE LETTERS

LATE REALIZATIONS

I always felt.
Unknowingly to myself, that
I had to be more than I was,
To be loved and appreciated.
But you saw me, and my weaknesses,
And still, called me perfect.
It felt uncomfortable.
So, I took it for granted.
I took *you* for granted,
I'm so sorry.
Sorry I couldn't accept your love.
I'd do anything to take it all back
To treat you better.
If you'd give me one last chance.
I'm willing to accept my fate.

REGRETS

I'm sorry for all the pain I've caused you.
God knows I love you,
God knows.
I'm sorry for
Throwing storms at you,
I know the pain I've caused you.

I'm sorry,
But sorry is not enough.

Anything to take away all the pain I've
caused you,
Being without you would be
the biggest tragedy.

I can't do without you.
You're my everything.

You're everything.
And I don't care what else is out there.

SEE

See, I want to love you
Be there for you
I don't know how to

Sometimes I don't know what loving
you means.
What does it look like?
Feel like,
How do I know it when I feel it?
How do I feel it?
Can I feel it?
Does it exist?

LETTING GO

It hasn't been easy, I can't let you go.
It kills,
To even try.
You're my everything.
You're my home.
Without you I feel lost
I need you.

HINDSIGHT

I know it was for the best,
But I can't forget the rest.
How did I leave such a mess?
Filled with regrets.

Make me forget the past
Thought we would last.

THICK WALLS

When she left, I thought,
"I didn't give you the piece of me I
couldn't live without,"
 Like I did last time, with her...
"You can go. I'll live."

GRATITUDE

Thank you for staying. If you enjoyed reading this, feel free to share your experience with others.

To order more copies, visit:
www.mysaneinsanity.ca

Instagram : Ditales_

www.ditalescreations.com

Creative Team (Instagram)

1. Author & Creative Director: DiTales_

2. Photography: Boyyu_

3. Illustration: peterdssbide